Fiona French studied Art Education at Croydon College of Art and went on to work as Bridget Riley's assistant. In 1970 she began a distinguished career as an illustrator and won the Kate Greenaway Medal for *Snow White in New York* in 1986. Among her titles for Frances Lincoln are *Little Inchkin, Lord of the Animals, Pepi and the Secret Names* (written by Jill Paton Walsh), which was shortlisted for the 1995 Children's Book Award, and *Jamil's Clever Cat.* Fiona lives in Aylsham, Norfolk.

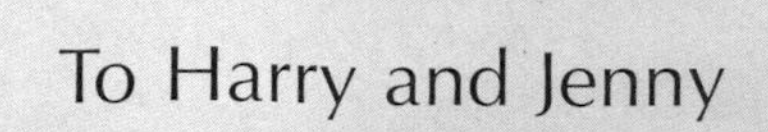

To Harry and Jenny

First published in Great Britain in 1991 by
Frances Lincoln Limited, 4 Torriano Mews
Torriano Avenue, London NW5 2RZ

First paperback edition 1992

British Library Cataloguing in Publication Data
available on request

ISBN 0-7112-0672-4 hardback
ISBN 0-7112-0787-9 paperback

Printed in Hong Kong

15 14 13 12 11 10 9 8

ANANCY
AND
MR DRY~BONE
FIONA FRENCH

FRANCES LINCOLN

Mr Dry-Bone lived in a big house
on top of a hill.
He was very rich and he wanted
to marry Miss Louise.

7 up

Anancy lived in a small house
at the foot of the hill.
He was very poor and he wanted to
marry Miss Louise as well.

Miss Louise lived on the other side of the hill.
She wasn't rich and she wasn't poor.
She was very clever and very very beautiful.
But Miss Louise had never laughed
in her whole life, so the first man
who could make her laugh,
that was the one she'd marry.

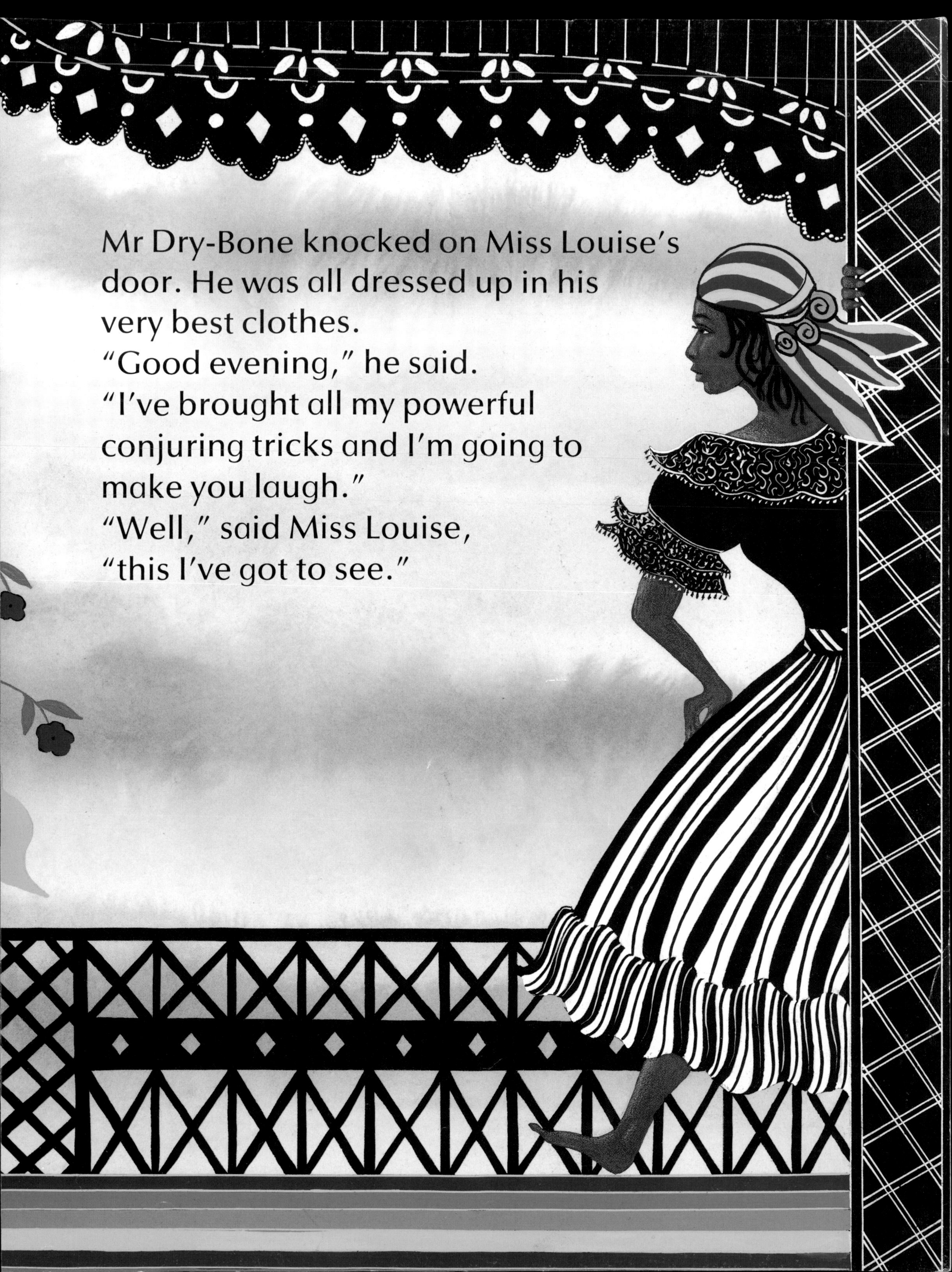

Mr Dry-Bone knocked on Miss Louise's door. He was all dressed up in his very best clothes.
"Good evening," he said.
"I've brought all my powerful conjuring tricks and I'm going to make you laugh."
"Well," said Miss Louise, "this I've got to see."

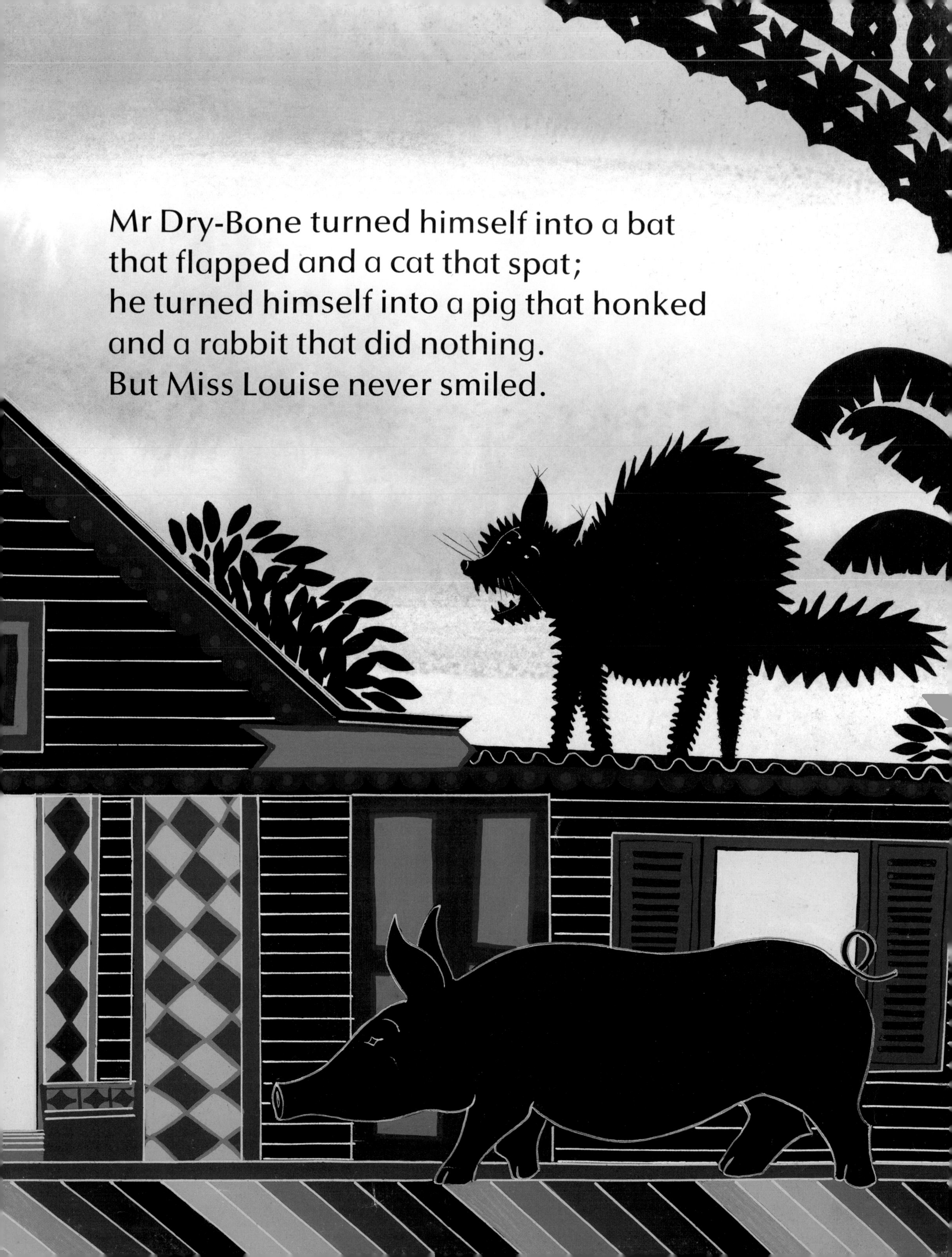

Mr Dry-Bone turned himself into a bat
that flapped and a cat that spat;
he turned himself into a pig that honked
and a rabbit that did nothing.
But Miss Louise never smiled.

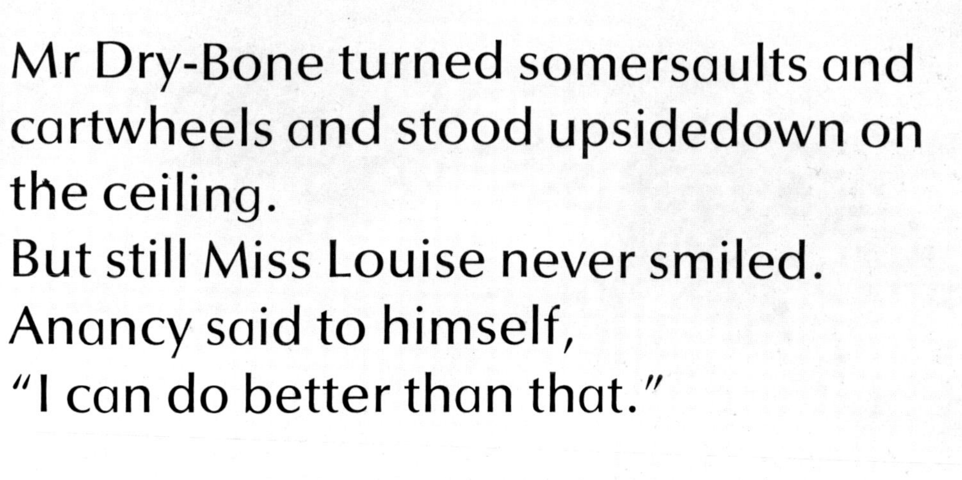

Mr Dry-Bone turned somersaults and cartwheels and stood upsidedown on the ceiling.
But still Miss Louise never smiled.
Anancy said to himself,
"I can do better than that."

Anancy went to Tiger and said,
"Lend me your best evening suit,
I'm going to visit Miss Louise."
Tiger said, "My evening suit
is at the cleaners right now,
but you can borrow my jogging suit."

Anancy went to see Dog.
"Lend me your top hat,
I'm going to visit Miss Louise."
Dog said, "My top hat got
crushed the other day but
you can borrow my
hunting hat."

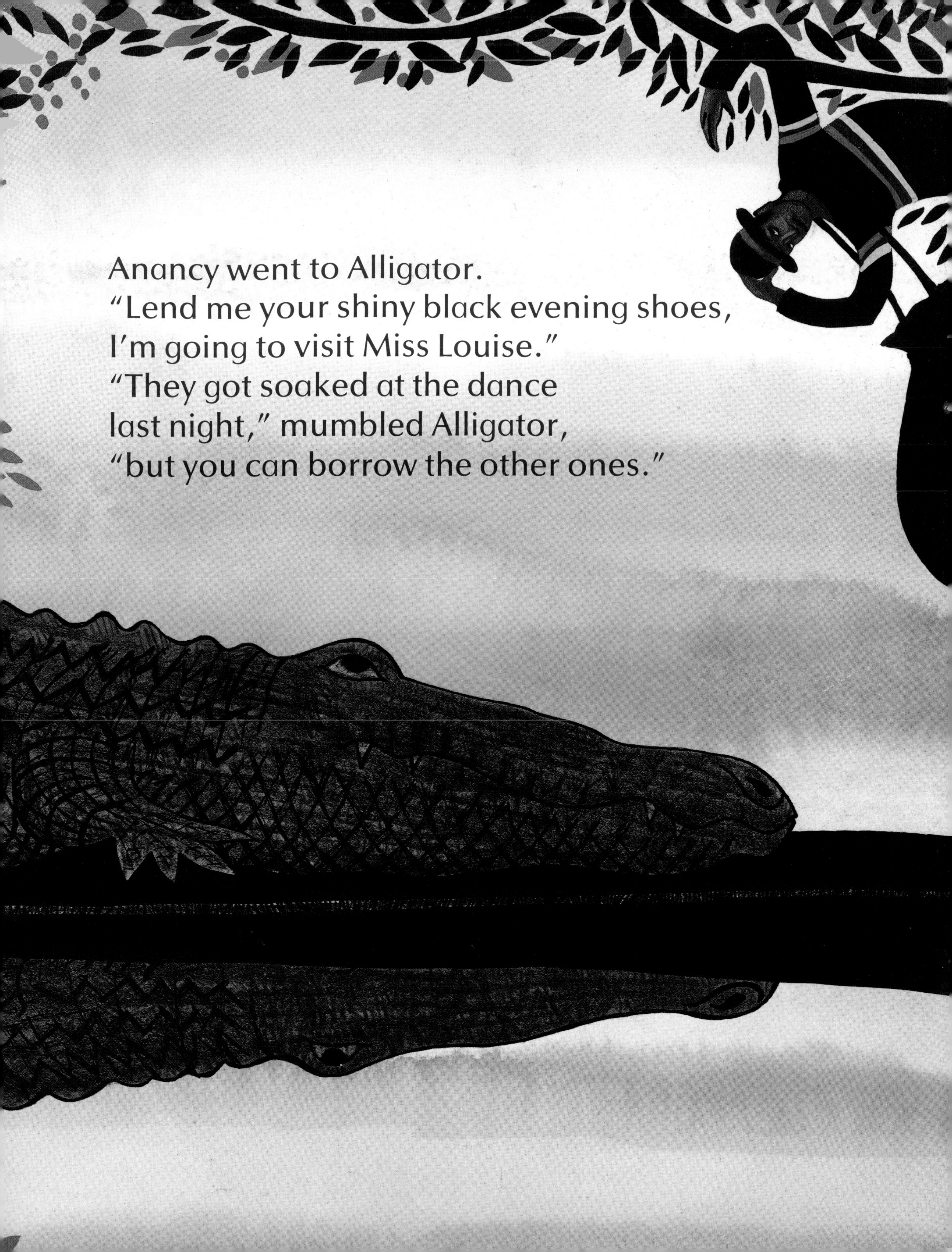

Anancy went to Alligator.
"Lend me your shiny black evening shoes,
I'm going to visit Miss Louise."
"They got soaked at the dance
last night," mumbled Alligator,
"but you can borrow the other ones."

Monkey swung through the trees
and called to Anancy,
"You'll need a tie when you
visit Miss Louise."

Parrot squawked and dropped
some feathers.
"Put these in your hunting hat, Anancy,
they'll look real good when you
visit Miss Louise."

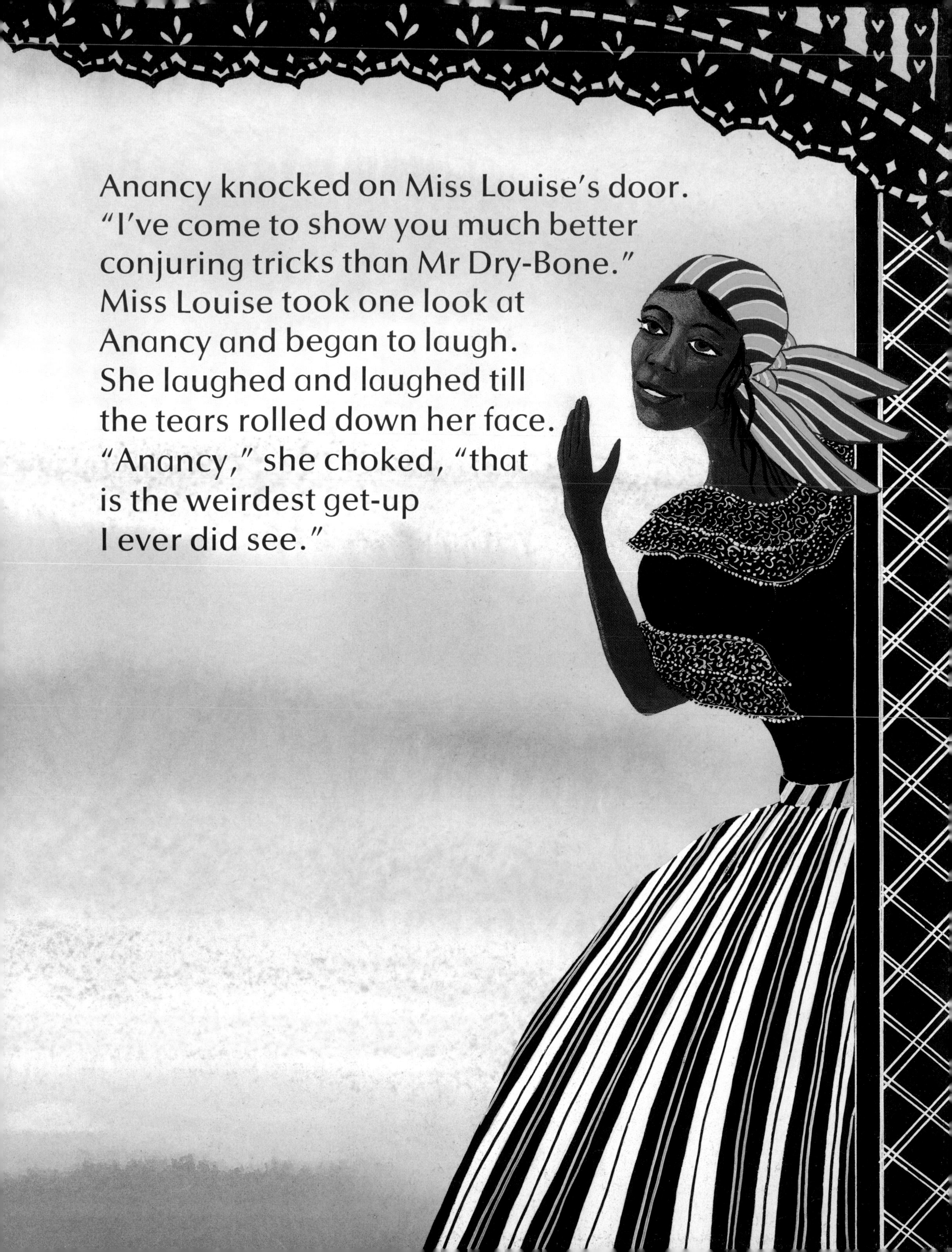

Anancy knocked on Miss Louise's door.
"I've come to show you much better conjuring tricks than Mr Dry-Bone."
Miss Louise took one look at Anancy and began to laugh.
She laughed and laughed till the tears rolled down her face.
"Anancy," she choked, "that is the weirdest get-up I ever did see."

Everyone laughed.
Even Mr Dry-Bone.
"OK, you win," he said.

So Anancy married Miss Louise,
and they all lived happily
ever after.

MORE PICTURE BOOKS IN PAPERBACK FROM FRANCES LINCOLN

PEPI AND THE SECRET NAMES

Jill Paton Walsh

Illustrated by Fiona French

Pepi's father is commanded to decorate a splendid tomb for Prince Dhutmose, with paintings of unimaginable creatures. Pepi decides to find his father real-life models of the animals, using his knowledge of secret names. . .

Suitable for National Curriculum English - Reading, Key Stage 2; History, Key Stage 2
Scottish Guidelines English Language - Reading, Levels C and D; Environmental Studies, Levels C and D

ISBN 0-7112-1089-6 £5.99

LITTLE INCHKIN

Fiona French

Little Inchkin is only as big as a lotus flower, but he has the courage of a Samurai warrior. How he proves his valour and wins the hand of a beautiful princess is charmingly retold in this Tom Thumb legend of old Japan.

Suitable for National Curriculum English - Reading, Key Stages 1 and 2
Scottish Guidelines English Language - Reading, Levels B and C

ISBN 0-7112-0917-0 £4.99

CHINYE

Obi Onyefulu

Illustrated by Evie Safarewicz

Poor Chinye! Back and forth through the forest she goes, fetching and carrying for her cruel stepmother. But strange powers are watching over her, and soon her life will be magically transformed... An enchanting retelling of a traditional West African folk tale of goodness, greed and a treasure-house of gold.

Suitable for National Curriculum English - Reading, Key Stages 1 and 2
Scottish Guidelines English Language - Reading, Levels B and C

ISBN 0-7112-1052-7 £4.99